Walt Disney's
Winnie the Pooh
and the Very Big Bear

Written by Joan Phillips
Illustrated by Bill Langley
and Diana Wakeman

A Golden Book • New York
Western Publishing Company, Inc., Racine, Wisconsin 53404

ISBN:0-307-11593-3/ISBN: 0-307-62593-1 (lib. bdg.)   MCMXC

Winnie the Pooh
wanted to go
fishing.
Rabbit and Piglet
wanted to go, too.

"We will go as soon
as the sun comes up,"
said Piglet.
"But how will *you*
get up, Pooh?"
asked Rabbit.

"The sun will
make me get up,"
said Pooh.
"The sun comes
in my window."
"Good!" said Rabbit.
"Good!" said Piglet.
"Good night!" said Pooh.

Pooh went into his house.

He got into bed.
Then he went right
to sleep.

A very big bear
stopped by Pooh's house.

He went right to sleep, too.

In the morning
the sun could not
come in.
Pooh did not
get up.

Rabbit and Piglet
sat and sat.
But Pooh did not come.

"We have to go
and get Pooh,"
said Piglet.
Rabbit and Piglet
ran to Pooh's house.

"We have to make
that bear go away,"
said Piglet.
"I will try,"
said Rabbit.

Rabbit tried.
But the bear did not
get up.
He did not go away.

"I will make the bear
go away,"
said Piglet.
Piglet tried.
But the bear did not
get up.
He did not go away.

"What will we do?"
said Rabbit and Piglet.

Inside the house
Pooh got up.
He did not see
the sun.

"Where is the sun?"
asked Pooh.
"What is that
in my window?"

"The sun is here,"
said Piglet.
"But there is a bear
at your window.
He will not
get up."

"I know what to do,"
said Pooh.
He gave Piglet
his honey.

Piglet and Rabbit
put the honey
on the ground.

The bear got up
at last.
He went far away.
He did not come back.

Then the sun came
into Pooh's house.

Pooh jumped up.
He went outside.

"Now we can all
go fishing,"
said Winnie the Pooh.
And they did.